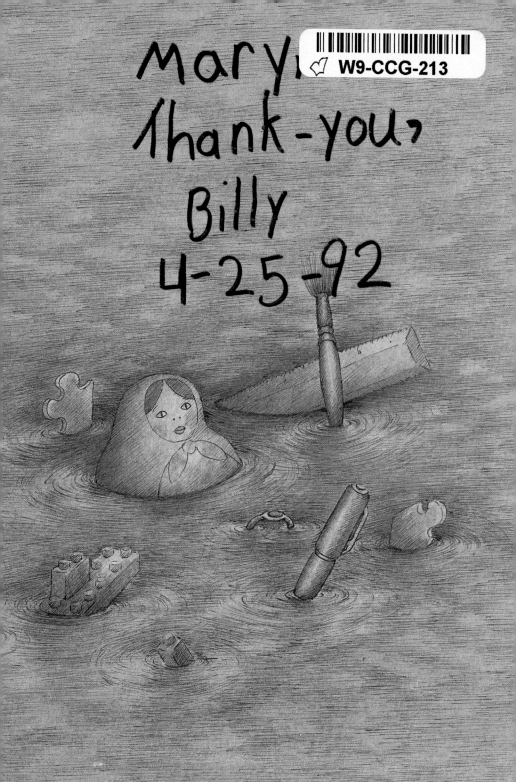

Mary
Thank-you,
Billy
4-25-92

For Graham
RI

For Helen
MK

First edition for the United States
and Canada published 1989 by
Barrons Educational Series, Inc.

Designed by Herman Lelie
Produced by Mathew Price Ltd
Old Rectory House
Marston Magna
Yeovil BA22 8DT
Somerset, England

International Standard Book No. 0-8120-5973-5

Library of Congress Catalog Card No. 89-350

Library of Congress Cataloging-in-Publication Data

Impey, Rose.
    The ankle grabber/Rose Impey: illustrated by Moira Kemp.
    – 1st ed.
(Creepies)
    Summary: Convinced that a monster Ankle Grabber lives in
a marsh under her bed, a little girl refuses to get out of bed until
her Dad finally scares the monster away.
    (1. Monsters – Fiction. 2. Night – Fiction. 3. Fear – Fiction.)
I. Kemp. Moira, ill. II. Title. III. Series.
PZ7. 1344An 1989 (E) – dc19
ISBN 0-8120-5973-5
                                                    89-350

Printed in Singapore

9012 987654321

Creepies

The Ankle Grabber

Rose Impey
Illustrated by Moira Kemp

BARRON'S

NEW YORK

Every night
when I go upstairs
my mom has to check out
the whole room
before I get into bed
and turn off the light.

First she draws back the curtains
to make sure that
The Flat Man
isn't hiding there,
pressed back
against the window
ready to slide out
and get me
when the light goes off.

Then she looks carefully
through the closet
in case Jumble Joan
is hanging there,
soft and lumpy,
pretending to be
a harmless set
of old clothes.

And last of all
she gets down
on her hands and knees
to search for
The Ankle Grabber,
who lives in the invisible swamp
just beneath my bed.

Even when Mom tells me,
"It's all clear,"
I can never be quite sure.
I peep around the door,
then make a quick dash
and jump onto my bed
from the middle of the room.

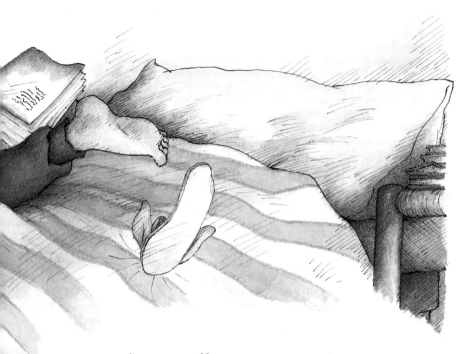

I try to keep well away
from the grabbing hand
which might shoot out
any minute,
pulling me
by my ankles —
down
down
down
into the sticky swamp,
never to be seen again.

Then I pull the covers
up to my nose
and peep over them
around the room.

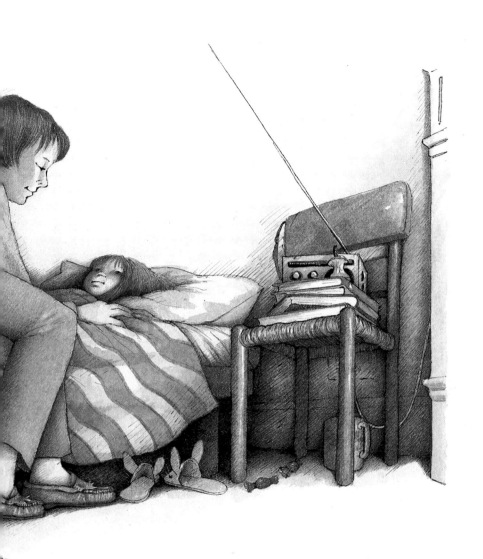

My mom shakes her head.
She says, "I've told you before,
there aren't any monsters
in this house."
Then she kisses me goodnight
and goes downstairs.

I lie in bed
all alone
in the dark
and my head
feels full of monsters.

I think of The Chimney Creeper
and The Guitar Gobbler,
but most of all
I think about
The Awful Ankle Grabber.

I think about
its two beady eyes
rolling
like glass marbles
from side to side
in its hooded head.

They peer out
above the swamp
always on the lookout
for anything
which might fall its way.

And I think about
its grasping hands
with their lizard-like fingers
reaching out
on long scaly arms
to get me.

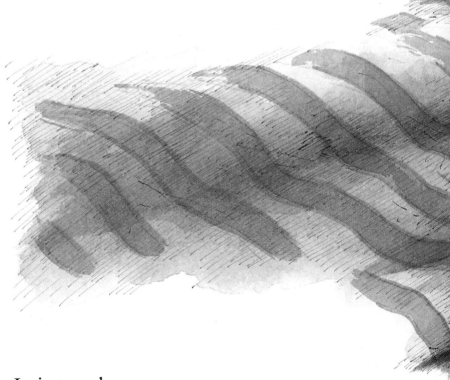

I picture them
curling their fingertips
as they climb
up the side of my bed,

creeping nearer and nearer
until they are almost
touching me.

I shiver
and squeeze myself
as thin as I can
into the very middle of the bed.
I tell myself,
if I stay there
without moving
I will be safe.

The Ankle Grabber can't get me
because it's stuck
in its slimy swamp.
No matter how much
it stretches
and struggles,
it can't get out.

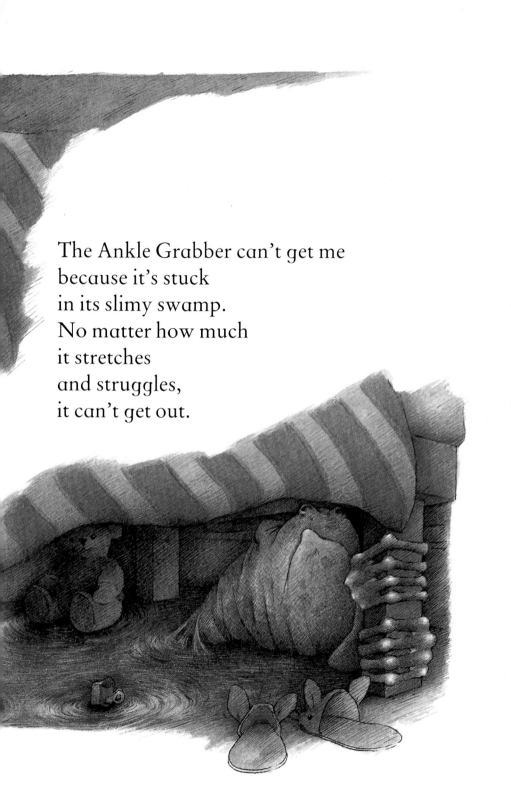

And I picture it
sinking back
into the mud
which boils and bubbles
around its ears,
sucking it down

until only two glassy eyes
are left,
waiting and watching
in the dark.

I turn over
and over,
rolling myself up
in the covers
like a huge jelly roll.
I hate it
lying there
wide awake
with my head full of monsters.

Then another horrible thought
creeps into my brain.
I start to think
I have to go to the bathroom!

I lie there
and I tell myself,
"I don't need to go,"
but I know I do.
I tell myself,
"I can wait
till the morning,"
but I know I can't.

I try to think about
something else
but all I can think of is
rain
and waterfalls
and dripping faucets
and in the end
I know I've got to go.

I take a deep breath
and make a jump
in the dark.

I land softly
near the door,
tiptoe along the landing,
and go into the bathroom.

Then I make a run
all the way back

and take a wild leap
into the room
flying through the air,
arms stretched out
like an eagle.

But I miss.
I hit the floor
with a BANG,

landing face down on the carpet
with my head
almost under the bed.

I hardly dare to look
in case I see
The Ankle Grabber
watching me.
Any minute his scaly hand
could shoot out and grab hold of me.

But then, when I do look,
I see someone else's eye
staring back at me.
My teddy's sitting there
on top of the swamp.
I reach out
to save him
before he is sucked in
and lost forever.

Suddenly I stop dead.

Behind me
I can feel a large hand,
cold and rough,
closing around my ankle.

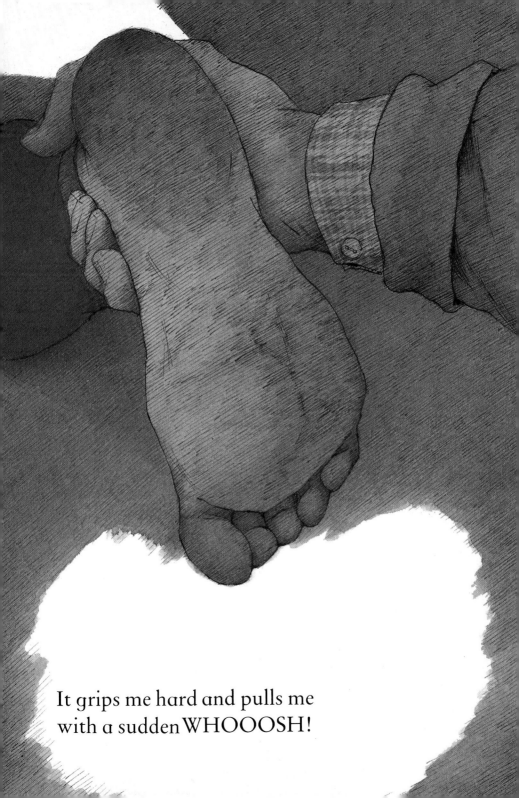

It grips me hard and pulls me
with a sudden WHOOOSH!

I feel myself sliding
along the bedroom floor.
I start to scream,
"Help! Mom, Dad! Help!"

"Now what are you doing
down there?" asks my dad.
I lie on my back
looking up at him
feeling pretty silly.
"I thought you were
The Ankle Grabber," I say.

"Oh, it's The Ankle Grabber tonight,"
says Dad. "Not The Terrible Toe Twiddler."
"No," I say, "not him."
"And The Nasty Knee Nibbler,
he hasn't been back?"
"No," I say. "You scared him off."

"Then it sounds to me
like another job
for The Dreadful Demon Dad."

"Look out," I call.
"My dad's coming to get you!"